TALENT SHOW MIX-UP

by Mickie Matheis
illustrated by Artful Doodlers

Grosset & Dunlap
An Imprint of Penguin Group (USA) Inc.

Used under license by Penguin Young Readers Group. All rights reserved. Published by Grosset & Dunlap, a division of Penguin Young Readers Group, 345 Hudson Street, New York, New York 10014. GROSSET & DUNLAP is a trademark of Penguin Group (USA) Inc. Printed in the U.S.A.

ISBN 978-0-448-45786-4   10 9 8 7 6 5 4 3 2 1

Have you heard of Zooble Isle? It's a magical world full of adorable Zoobles—little balls that pop open into fantastical creatures on their Happitats. There are many lands on Zooble Isle. Can you find them all on the map?

PETAGONIA

AZOOZIA

PINEGROVE

PETAL POINT

Zoobles love to spend time together and play all sorts of games.

They always have so much fun!

Zoobles magically transform when on top of their Happitats!

SEAGONIA

CHILLVILLE

One day, Zoobles from all over Zooble Isle came to Chillville, a snowy land full of cold-loving creatures, for a day of play.

"I love chilling out here!" said Fenton the Forest Fox. Fenton was from Pinegrove, a woodsy land with lots of pine trees. He was digging through the snow to create a hideout.

Some snow landed on Estelle the Starfish. Estelle was from Seagonia,
a splashy region under the sea.

"Did you know that no two snowflakes are alike?" she said. Estelle was
supersmart and knew all kinds of fun facts.

"Where are Ears and Flutter?" wondered Waddles, a penguin from Chillville. Just then, a big snowball nearby began to shake. Snow exploded everywhere as Ears the Bunny popped out. Ears was from Petagonia, the land of pets. "Surprise!" he shouted, hopping high into the air.

As soon as Ears landed, a snowball dropped from the sky and plopped down right between his ears. Flutter the Butterfly laughed and flew down. "Surprise to *you*!" he teased. Flutter was from Petal Point, a beautiful region full of colorful flowers and insects.

"All right, you two—game over," said Jaffa the Giraffe. Jaffa was from Azoozia, where zoo animals lived. She was very polite. She turned to Waddles and said, "Thank you for inviting us here today. We had a lovely time."

"It was *snow* much fun!" Flutter agreed. "Can you all pop in to visit me at Petal Point next? I thought we could have a talent show!"

"What's a talent show?" asked the other Zoobles with interest.

Of course, Estelle already knew the answer. "It's an event where everyone performs a special skill, and the audience votes for their favorite," she explained.

The Zoobles all thought it sounded like fun. They headed back to their regions on Zooble Isle to practice their talents for the show.

Ears was the highest hopper in Petagonia.

He went home to practice hopping high.

Jaffa had the longest neck in all of Azoozia.

She went home to stretch.

Fenton always found the best hiding places in Pinegrove.

He went home to practice hiding.

Estelle was the smartest Zooble in Seagonia.

She went home to read about Petal Point.

Waddles was the best designer in Chillville. She went home to create a beautiful costume.

Flutter already had a plan for what he was going to do.

Plus, he had to get things ready in Petal Point for the show.

The big day arrived. All the Zoobles gathered in front of the stage were excited for the show to begin.

Estelle was the first to take the stage. She asked the Zoobles to quiz her with questions about the flowers in Petal Point. How many grew there? Which was the biggest? Which had the softest petals? Estelle knew all the answers. The crowd clapped in amazement.

Ears came out next. He hopped high in the air and pulled a flower out from behind his back. He then landed on top of a giant mushroom, threw the flower into the crowd, and hopped back onto the stage. The audience was delighted.

Then it was Jaffa's turn. The Zoobles *ooh*ed and *aah*ed as she walked over to a tall flower on the side of the stage. She stretched her neck up, up, up until she reached some petals. She grabbed a mouthful as the crowd cheered.

Next up was Fenton. He appeared on the stage and then suddenly disappeared. He made funny noises, and the Zoobles realized that he was hiding behind a mushroom on the side of the stage! The audience yelled and stomped their feet.

"Fenton, my friend, that was clever—but watch this!" A voice boomed from the back of the stage. Flutter zoomed overhead and dropped flower petals on the audience. The Zoobles waved the petals wildly and whistled.

Finally it was Waddles's turn. Everyone waited for her to come out. But she had a problem: She couldn't find her costume!

"What will I do?" Waddles whimpered. She had worked so hard on her performance, and now she couldn't be in the show.

"Give me a minute!" Estelle said. She pulled herself into a ball and rolled around.
This was how she did her best thinking.

Suddenly she popped open on her Happitat and held up one of her arms. "I have
an idea!" she announced. "Petal Point is full of beautiful mushrooms, flowers, and
grass. Let's make a Petal Point costume for Waddles!"

The Zoobles sprang into action. Jaffa grabbed some grass and wove it around Waddles's waist. Flutter put a small mushroom on her head. Ears strung a bunch of flowers into a necklace and hung it around her neck. Fenton and Estelle covered her with more flowers.

When the Zoobles saw Waddles parade around in her beautiful costume, they clapped and cheered. Waddles was the clear winner of the talent show!

"Thank you!" Waddles said. "I couldn't have won without all of you!"

Waddles's friends gathered around her. "That's what friends are for—especially when we have a friend as cool as you, Waddles!"